THE CHURCH MICE SPREAD THEIR WINGS

Graham Oakley

M

SBN 333 18566 8

First published 1975 by
MACMILLAN LONDON LIMITED
London and Basingstoke
Associated companies in New York Dublin
Melbourne Johannesburg and Delhi

Printed in Great Britain by
COLOUR REPRODUCTIONS LIMITED

For my mother

Humphrey the Schoolmouse had been reading again, and one pleasant afternoon in Wortlethorpe Churchyard he began to lecture his fellow church mice. "We have become Victims of the Rat Race," he told them, "crushed by the Pressures of Modern Life. Our nerves are being torn to shreds in the Mad Struggle for Survival."

At this moment everyone went indoors for tea.

But during tea he started up again. "We must escape the Toils of Society," he declared. "We must seek the woods and fields where we can gambol amidst the buttercups and have our fevered brows soothed by the cool fingers of Mother Nature."

Just then a crumb went down the wrong way and his friend Arthur had to take over.

"A weekend in the country will do us all good," Arthur said. "And speaking as a practical sort of chap, I suggest a party leaves each Saturday morning, gets its fevered brow soothed and returns in time for tea on Sunday. Sampson will act as escort. He'll have to give up all his weekends, of course, but he won't mind."

Sampson woke up long enough to say he jolly well did mind, and then tried to get back to sleep. But by this time the mice had got Humphrey's message. They made it very clear that their Return to Nature was not to be spoiled by Sampson's selfishness.

As a church cat, Sampson had taken a solemn vow never to harm mice, so there was nothing he could do but agree. On thinking it over, however, he wasn't too depressed. Mice being mice, it seemed possible that the first outing might be the last. All the same he made a secret wish that something terrible would happen, just to be on the safe side.

That evening Arthur organized the drawing of lots to make up the first party and Humphrey brought out his map and explained exactly where they would be going.

The following morning they set off early. In stretches the going was a little rough. But even a church cat has his pride, and when the mice were out of danger and Arthur said, "Now you see why I brought you, old chap," Sampson did not reply. He just wondered what happened to cats that broke vows.

When they reached the river bank they began to enjoy the peace and quiet of the countryside.

After they had enjoyed quite a lot of peace and quiet, Arthur, who had found a boat, suggested a river trip. Everyone thought this a splendid idea, even Sampson, though something made him faintly uneasy. He couldn't think quite what.

But it wasn't long before he remembered.

Luckily everyone held on tight, because when they surfaced they found themselves being tossed by gigantic waves. "We've been washed out to sea! All is lost!" shrieked the mice. However in due course their boat hit a rock and they were able to struggle ashore.

"When Mother Nature has finished soothing our fevered brows perhaps she could give us a good rubdown as well," said Sampson bitterly as they stood dripping by the water's edge. This made Humphrey very angry. "Here we are, cast up on a foreign and exotic shore and all you can do is make silly jokes," he snapped, studying the map which had got a little damp.

"According to my calculations, we're in China,"
he said, "probably on the Pong Yang Peninsula."
"We're in Wortlethorpe Park," mumbled Sampson.

"Rubbish!" cried Humphrey. "Look over there.
We're in Chi . . . er . . . India! Cats know
nothing about Geography."

This was too much for Sampson. If the mice wanted a foreign and exotic shore they could have one. "Crumbs, you must be right! Here comes a Greater Spotted Indian Mouse-eater!" he cried. "Run for your lives!"

But they hadn't run far when he shouted, "Stop! A Lesser Scarlet Indian Mouse-swallowing Water Snake!"

With Mouse-eaters behind and Mouse-swallowers ahead, the mice were convinced their last hour had come. Sampson was heard to remark that creatures who were just walking dinners should have stayed at home in the vestry, but all the same he showed them a way to escape and they got past the Water Snake safely.

Then the jungle closed in. The mice grew more
and more tetchy and homesick. They said it
would be nice to see some proper British flowers
instead of these nasty, vulgar, foreign-looking
things. They glowered at Arthur and Humphrey
and grumbled about how they could have been having
a nice cosy tea now if it wasn't for some people's
rotten ideas about Mother Nature and weekend trips.

Finally Sampson, who never stayed bad-tempered
long, decided to take pity on the mice and lead them
home by a short cut he knew across the sandpits.
But as soon as he saw the sand Humphrey resumed
command. "My calculations are correct!" he
announced importantly. "We have reached the
Sahara Desert!"

Sampson pointed out a steeple and some oak trees and said that you didn't see many of those in the Sahara, but Humphrey only looked at him pityingly. "There are such things as mirages, you know," he said. "Deserts are full of them. Cats know nothing about Natural Science."

Sampson stopped feeling sorry for the mice and followed grimly along behind as Humphrey led them into the trackless wastes of the Sahara.

They were soon hot, thirsty and lost, and if Arthur hadn't spotted the oasis, there's no saying what might have happened to them.

But a drink and a dip soon made them feel better and they might all have succumbed to the Spell of the Desert if Humphrey hadn't insisted on giving a long lecture on *The Origins of Curious Rock Formations found by Humphrey in an Uncharted Region of the Sahara* . . .

. . . which didn't last as long as he'd intended.

"EARTHQUAKE!" shouted Arthur. "Every mouse for himself!" Fortunately there was only one way to run. The Sahara ended at the river where they scrambled onto a branch of driftwood because Humphrey said it was dangerous to stay on land in the vicinity of a seismic fault. "We are now in the Mediterranean Sea," he announced. "If we turn right at Gibraltar we should be home in time for dinner."

It took some time to cross the Mediterranean but eventually they reached the opposite shore. It seemed rather thickly populated, but they saw that someone had very kindly left a line for them to make fast to.

"Ahoy there, my man," shouted Humphrey. "Is this England?"

The man shouted back something rather rude but very British, so they knew they were home at last.

Once more on British soil, there were some very emotional scenes. Humphrey said a few words about Britannia welcoming her Wandering Sons back to her bosom, and Arthur hummed *Land of Hope and Glory*. Everyone agreed that now they'd seen the rest of the world, you couldn't beat good old England . . .

. . . except that it was rather late and beginning to rain. As the mice got colder and wetter they began to say that England was going to the dogs, and everyone agreed it was little wonder people emigrated and went abroad for holidays.

Then the rain stopped, the moon appeared, and everyone agreed that it was awfully nice to have a changeable climate and they couldn't understand why people went abroad at all.

Arthur and Humphrey stepped out into the open to take a quick bearing on the Pole Star and set a course for home. Humphrey was just remarking on how lovely it was to live in a country where a fellow could walk about at night in perfect safety when . . .

. . . an absolutely terrible thing happened.

At first they were too shaken to speak, but after a
while Humphrey said in a trembly kind of voice,
"Apropos of nothing, what do barn owls eat?"
  "Small mammals," said Arthur.
  "Ah . . . interesting," said Humphrey.

And after they'd flown a little further, Humphrey
said in a casual sort of tone, "Just for the sake of
conversation, how big, approximately speaking,
would you say 'small mammals' are?"
  "As big as us," said Arthur.
  "Ah . . . interesting," said Humphrey.

"Jolly decent of you to give us a lift home, old thing," he said. "We'd like to stay for a bit of a chin-wag, but it's past our bedtime so we ought to be toddling. Nightie-night, old sausage." They started to walk away, but they didn't get very far.

But when they saw that the owl had brought them to their own church tower, their spirits rose a little. Arthur decided to try the friendly approach.

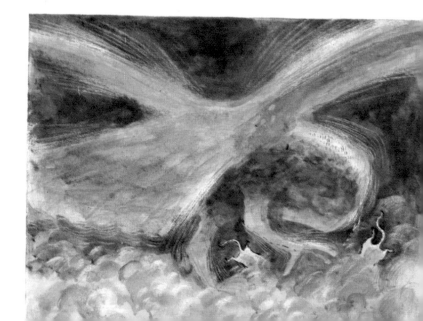

When the owl was sure they couldn't escape, it dropped off to sleep. The mice could not help feeling things looked a little bleak. Humphrey gave way to morbid reflections upon mortality, but Arthur passed the time more usefully.

They thought they had fooled the owl rather neatly, until they discovered that without mountaineering equipment there was no way out of the belfry.

The owl awoke feeling agreeably hungry. When it found that its claw was full of stones and its breakfast was attempting a getaway, it lost its temper completely.

They escaped by the skin of their teeth. The owl was beside itself, but it knew it only had to wait. There was no way out of the cupboard, either.

Humphrey became fatalistic. He said that the Hand of Destiny was raised against them, the Sands of Time had run out, the Book of Fate was closed and there was no use fighting against what was Written in the Stars. "Piffle!" said Arthur, because it jolly well wasn't written in the stars. He'd thought of a plan.

It took them the whole day. Luckily they found the remains of someone's fishpaste sandwich which kept them going. By nightfall everything was ready, but the owl had become very suspicious. They decided to wait until morning . . .

. . . when at last the owl finally nodded off. The sun was long up and they had almost abandoned hope, but it was now or never.

Humphrey muttered grumpily that if mice had been meant to fly they would have been born with wings, but he was only jealous because it was Arthur's idea.

It's a short, pleasant journey from the church to the parsonage .

. but the way they went was neither short nor pleasant.

And when they arrived, they were not at all welcome. The parson pointed out that as prominent church mice they were supposed to set a good example. Much more of this sort of thing, he said severely, and no gentleman of the cloth would be able to take a well-earned glass of port without finding half a dozen mice frisking about in it.

He demanded to know which of them was responsible for such a foolish, hare-brained prank, and without any hesitation they told him.

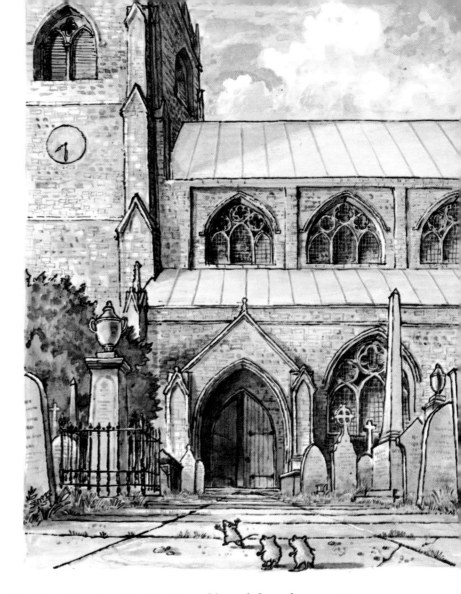

And while they had a bit of breakfast, he went on with the talking-to. After that he sent them packing back to the vestry. On the way they met a friend. Somehow his greeting seemed a bit odd.

in mamory of humfri and arther
taken abuv last saterday nite
in the flour of there yuth

from all in the vestry
with lots of luv xxx

SAMPSON

JORICE ALLSORTS

They soon saw why. At first everyone was terrified, but when they realized that it really was Arthur and Humphrey and not their ghosts, everyone turned very nasty. They said that the two mice were a pair of wet blankets for showing up in the middle of their own funeral and spoiling all the fun. After a while, however, they calmed down, particularly as something had to be done about the food, so they had a party instead of a funeral and ended up enjoying themselves in spite of the disappointment.

As for Sampson, he was quite pleased to see the mice again. He had been feeling that their frightful fate was all his fault because of his secret wish that something terrible would happen, so it was a weight off his conscience when they turned up alive and fairly well.

Best of all, their adventures were sure to put an end once and for all to the whole idea of weekend jaunts. Sampson had a drowsy feeling that the mice of Wortlethorpe Church would resist the Mad Pressures of the Rat Race without further help from Mother Nature, and pleased with his own sagacity, resourcefulness and patience, he drifted off into a peaceful snooze at last.